Mademoiselle Moon

First published in paperback in 2007

Published in Canada by Fitzhenry & Whiteside,
195 Allstate Parkway, Markham, Ontario L3R 4T8

Published in the United States by Fitzhenry & Whiteside,
311 Washington Street, Brighton, Massachusetts 02135

www.fitzhenry.ca   godwit@fitzhenry.ca

10 9 8 7 6 5 4 3 2 1

Library and Archives Canada Cataloguing in Publication
Gay, Marie-Louise
Mademoiselle Moon / Marie-Louise Gay.
First published: Toronto : Stoddart, 1992.
ISBN-13: 978-1-55005-134-6
ISBN-10: 1-55005-134-2
I. Title.
PS8563.A868M34 2006   jC813'.54   C2006-903457-5

U.S. Publisher Cataloging-in-Publication Data
(Library of Congress Standards)

Gay, Marie-Louise.
Mademoiselle Moon / Marie-Louise Gay.
Originally published: 1992.
[32] p. : col. ill. ; cm.
Summary: The extraordinary tale about love and friendship between Mademoiselle Moon and Mister Sun.
ISBN-10: 1-55005-134-2 (pbk.)
ISBN-13: 978-1-55005-134-6 (pbk.)
1. Friendship – Fiction – Juvenile literature. 2. Love – Fiction – Juvenile literature.   I. Title.
[E] dc22   PZ7.G556MA 2006

Fitzhenry & Whiteside acknowledges with thanks the Canada Council for the Arts, and the Ontario Arts Council
for their support of our publishing program. We acknowledge the financial support of the Government of Canada
through the Book Publishing Industry Development Program (BPIDP) for our publishing activities.

 Canada Council
for the Arts   Conseil des Arts
du Canada   ONTARIO ARTS COUNCIL
CONSEIL DES ARTS DE L'ONTARIO

Printed in Hong Kong

Mademoiselle Moon

Written and Illustrated
by
Marie-Louise Gay

Fitzhenry & Whiteside

For Christa

Mister Sun and Mademoiselle Moon
were old friends.
They had known each other
since the dawn of time.
When Mister Sun was born,
Mademoiselle Moon
was there to greet him.
She helped him climb
out of his shell
and they danced the night away...

Flowers grew and waves
splashed high on the moonlit
shores.
Lizards crawled out and smiled
their secret lizard smiles.
Fireflies blinked and dolphins
jumped.
The air smelt of banana cream
and roses. Then Mister Sun
and Mademoiselle Moon went
their separate ways.
Each had a job to do.

For years and years they only caught glimpses of each other. Sometimes, on a warm spring evening, Mademoiselle Moon would appear, a soft pale face in the golden sky.
She would wave to Mister Sun as he slipped behind the mountains to his bed.

Other times, as Mister Sun
emerged in the cool wintry
dawn, yawning and shivering,
he would see Mademoiselle
Moon gliding home after a
long night's work.
Like a lovely firefly, she would
disappear in a wink between
the trees of the forest.
They missed each other a lot.

But one gray, drizzly morning, they met again.
It was Mister Sun's day off.
"Mademoiselle Moon!" cried Mister Sun. "It's been so long! How are you?"
"Not so well," said Mademoiselle Moon. " I feel old and useless. After all these years, I've lost my job! Another moon is starting tonight."
"How terrible!" said Mister Sun. "But still, there are so many things you could do. You could become a doctor or a dancer or... or a pilot or a ..."

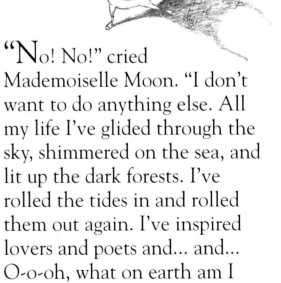

"No! No!" cried Mademoiselle Moon. "I don't want to do anything else. All my life I've glided through the sky, shimmered on the sea, and lit up the dark forests. I've rolled the tides in and rolled them out again. I've inspired lovers and poets and... and... O-o-oh, what on earth am I going to do now?"

"Don't you worry," said Mister Sun. "You are my best friend. I will help you."

It had stopped raining and the clouds were gently drifting apart.

"Uh-oh!" said Mister Sun. "It looks like I've got a bit of work to do after all. Wait for me here – I'll be back at dusk."

With that, Mister Sun took a deep breath, dove into the sea, and swam swiftly towards the horizon.

Mademoiselle Moon sighed as she opened her umbrella and sat down to wait and wait and wait.

Hours later, Mademoiselle Moon awoke with a start. "Stars and planets!" she exclaimed. "This is going to be quite a storm!"
There was a tremendous clap of thunder. Lightning forked across the sky and waves pounded the beach. Then Mademoiselle Moon saw the lighthouse. She ran towards it, tugged at the door, and dashed in. It was dark and safe and quiet.

A staircase spiraled up into
the darkness. Mademoiselle
Moon started climbing. Round
and round. Higher and higher.
As she neared the top, she
heard a voice say,
"Finally! There you are! I've
been waiting for you!"
In a shadowy room sat a small
fat man warming his feet by a
stove.
"Please sit down and have
some tea," said the man.

"How could you be waiting for me?" asked Mademoiselle Moon. "I don't even know you."

"I've known you forever," said the man. "I've seen you play hide and seek with the clouds. I've seen you thin as a toenail clipping and fat as a Halloween pumpkin. I'm the lighthouse keeper and... I need your help."

"Me?" said Mademoiselle Moon. "How can I help you?"

"I just can't manage those stairs anymore," said the lighthouse keeper. "And with this storm I know there will be a disaster..." Just then there was a crack of thunder.

KAA-BOOM!

"Please help me..." he said.
"Oh well, I suppose I could
try..." As she climbed the last
set of stairs to the very top,
Mademoiselle Moon grumbled,
"I don't know anything about
lighthouses."
She examined the lantern.
"Just as I thought! I'll never
understand how this works."
There was a tremendous flash
of lightning
and Mademoiselle Moon
caught a glimpse of a
small boat bouncing closer
and closer to the rocks.

"Oh no!" cried Mademoiselle
Moon. "It's going to crash!
What can I do?" She paced
the floor and wrung
her hands in despair.
Then she stopped
and smiled....

Mademoiselle Moon
spent the rest of the dark
stormy night glowing with
happiness. And all the boats
came safely back to shore.

At dawn, Mister Sun emerged from the sea, slick and shiny as a seal.

"Mademoiselle Moon! It looks like you found a new job after all!"

"Maybe..." said Mademoiselle Moon, "... and we could see each other every day, couldn't we?"

Mister Sun blushed. The clouds turned bright pink.

"You are the lighthouse keeper, aren't you?" asked Mademoiselle Moon.

"I *was*," answered Mister Sun, "but that's *your* job now."